Butterfly Mornings

DEDICATED TO YOU. . .

Beautiful you are
in each and
every way.
Just as a butterfly —
each rainbow, each day.

Thanks for This Beautiful Day

Butterfly Mornings,
and warm, sunshiny days,
Happiness and beauty
We'll search for today.

We'll pick flowers for God
and talk to Him, too,
While we discover our world
and find new things to do.

Whistling a tune
and swinging up high,
We'll giggle and laugh
as we reach for the sky.

I looked in mom's garden,
and what did I see –
Sweet baby flowers
smiling back at me.

One small daisy
and a beautiful red rose,
Two tiny buttercups
tickling my toes.

Searching for wild berries
along a wooded path,
We'll fill our buckets full and
remember to save mom half.

I'll find a new friend,
maybe two, three, or four,
Then I'll open my heart –
where there's room for lots more.

Their skin might be different –
yellow, red, white, or brown,
But I'll look in their heart,
where true friends are found.

There's very little difference,
between them and me,
We've got the same stuff
as far as I can see.

We all have two ears,
two eyes and one nose,
We all have ten fingers
and ten tiny little toes.

Two arms and two feet,
one funny shaped-head,
We all have one mouth,
that likes to be fed.

A brain that can think
and a heart full of love,
A body that smells
if we don't scrub in the tub.

We'll play with our friends
until time for lunch,
Then we'll head straight for home
for something to munch.

My mouth starts to water
as we enter the door.
It's Grandma's famous pot roast,
mashed potatoes and more!

We'll eat homemade bread
and old-fashioned pumpkin pie,
Strawberries and cream
and nuts piled high.

After lunch it's time
to be up, up and away.
"GOODIE, GOODIE, GUMDROPS,"
We're off – to run, jump and play.

We'll fish and sit on fences,
and blow bubbles in the wind,
Make mud pies, and jump in puddles
sell lemonade and play pretend.

Fresh fruit and wild flowers
We'll pick along the way,
Run laughing through showers
on this rainbow-filled day.

For an afternoon snack,
we'll eat something sweet,
I hear the ice cream man now
He's on the next street.

He sells Nutty Buddies®
and Dreamsicles® too,
I'll give you first pick
For a bite off your stick!

Let's make funny faces
and fly kites in the sky,
chase butterflies and each other
and dream of Aunt Bea's apple pie.

Ring a ding ding

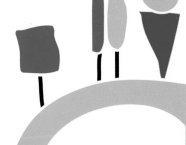

ICE CREAM

We'll see blue jays building nests
where their new babies will rest,
and watch squirrels frolic and play
hiding nuts along the way.

We'll see bees busy making honey
as we skip and feel free.
We'll eat cherries and sing,
as we climb up a tree.

Then we'll lie on the grass
and search for fuzzy things that crawl.
We'll dig for wiggling worms
and look for bugs climbing up the wall.

Butterfly Mornings

At the end of the day,
we'll build a tent for the night,
roast hot dogs and marshmallows
till they're brown and just right!

We'll tell scary stories
and share our secrets too.
We'll snuggle together as the
fire warms me and you.

Now it's the end of the day
and we're exhausted from our play,
So let's close our eyes, and slip away,
and dream of another –
"Butterfly Morning"
now on it's way.

By **CHARACTER BUILDERS** For kids

(407) 677-7171 Phone
(407) 677-1010 Fax

©Copyright 1997 Bonnie L. Sosé

ISBN# 0-9615279-8-6